Published in the United States by Grolier Enterprises Inc.,
Danbury, Connecticut. Originally published in Denmark by
Egmont Gruppen, Copenhagen.

ISBN: 0-7172-8795-5

Manufactured in the United States of America.
A B C D   1 2 3 4

WALT DISNEY'S
OLIVER
& Company

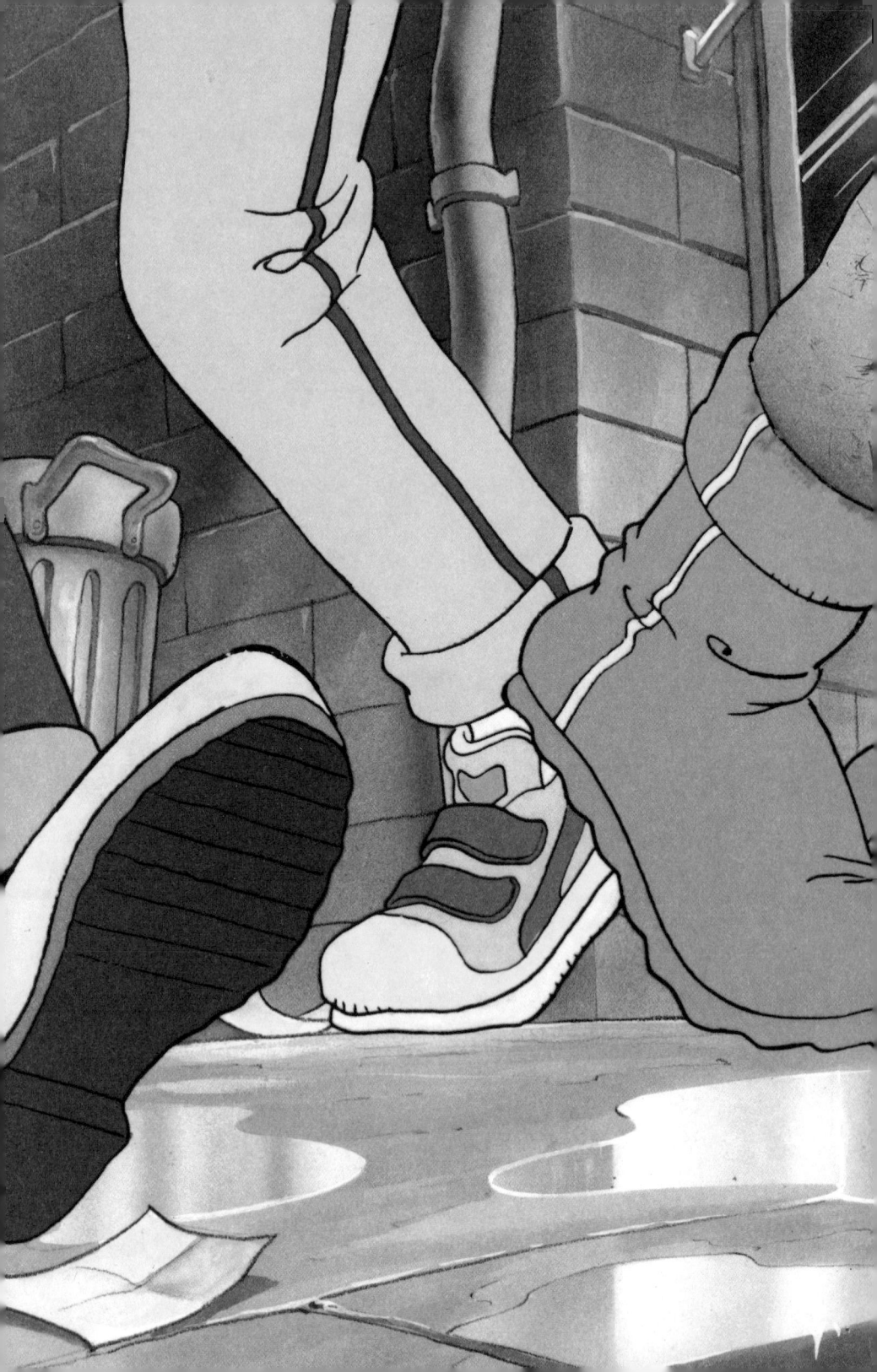

Early one morning a box full of kittens was left on a busy New York street. Soon all the kittens but one had been adopted. The last kitten was frightened, cold, and hungry.

Suddenly it started to rain. As the kitten ran for shelter, he was almost trampled by people rushing to work.

If only he had a home or some friends to
help him! But just then the kitten smelled
a most wonderful smell of steaming sausages.

The kitten was very hungry. He didn't think the man would mind if he took a bit of sausage.

The man did not want to share. He grabbed the kitten and rolled him down the street like a bowling ball!

The kitten bumped and tumbled along the street. He crashed to a stop. When he opened his eyes he saw a big dog. The kitten began to tremble.

"Take it easy," the dog said to the kitten. "My name's Dodger, and I don't eat cats. They have too much fur."

"Let's work together," Dodger continued. "I'll show you how to get sausages."

"Not me!" cried the kitten. "I'm not going back there!"

But Dodger wasn't listening. He wanted the kitten to help him distract the man. So Dodger began to bark and chase the startled kitten.

The kitten and dog raced toward the cart. When the kitten had nowhere else to go, he jumped onto the man's back! As the man tried to pull the cat off, Dodger snatched a string of sausages.

"I told you to leave everything to me," Dodger said as he bounded away.

"Not so fast!" called the kitten. "Wait for me!"

Dodger stopped only long enough to grab a pair of sunglasses from a table. Then he sped away again.

"Bye, bye, cat!"
Dodger cried, leaping
onto a taxi.

But the kitten
shouted, "Come
back! Those are my
sausages, too! It's not fair!"

"Fairs are for tourists!" called Dodger, jumping onto the back of a speeding motorcycle.

In spite of the dog's efforts, the brave little cat followed him to the docks. There he saw Dodger boarding a shabby houseboat.

The kitten scampered aboard the boat and climbed onto the roof. He could see Dodger with some other dogs— and his sausages, too!

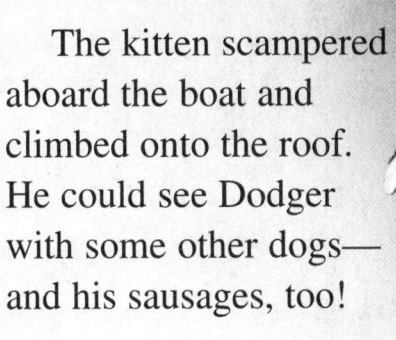

"Look, dinner!" Dodger boasted to the dogs. "And I had to fight off a horrible monster with long claws and razor-sharp teeth to get it!"

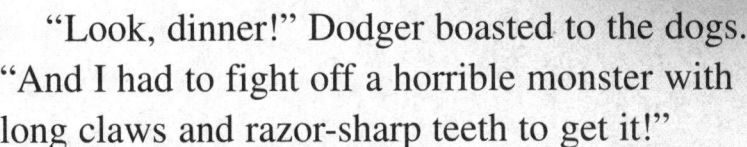

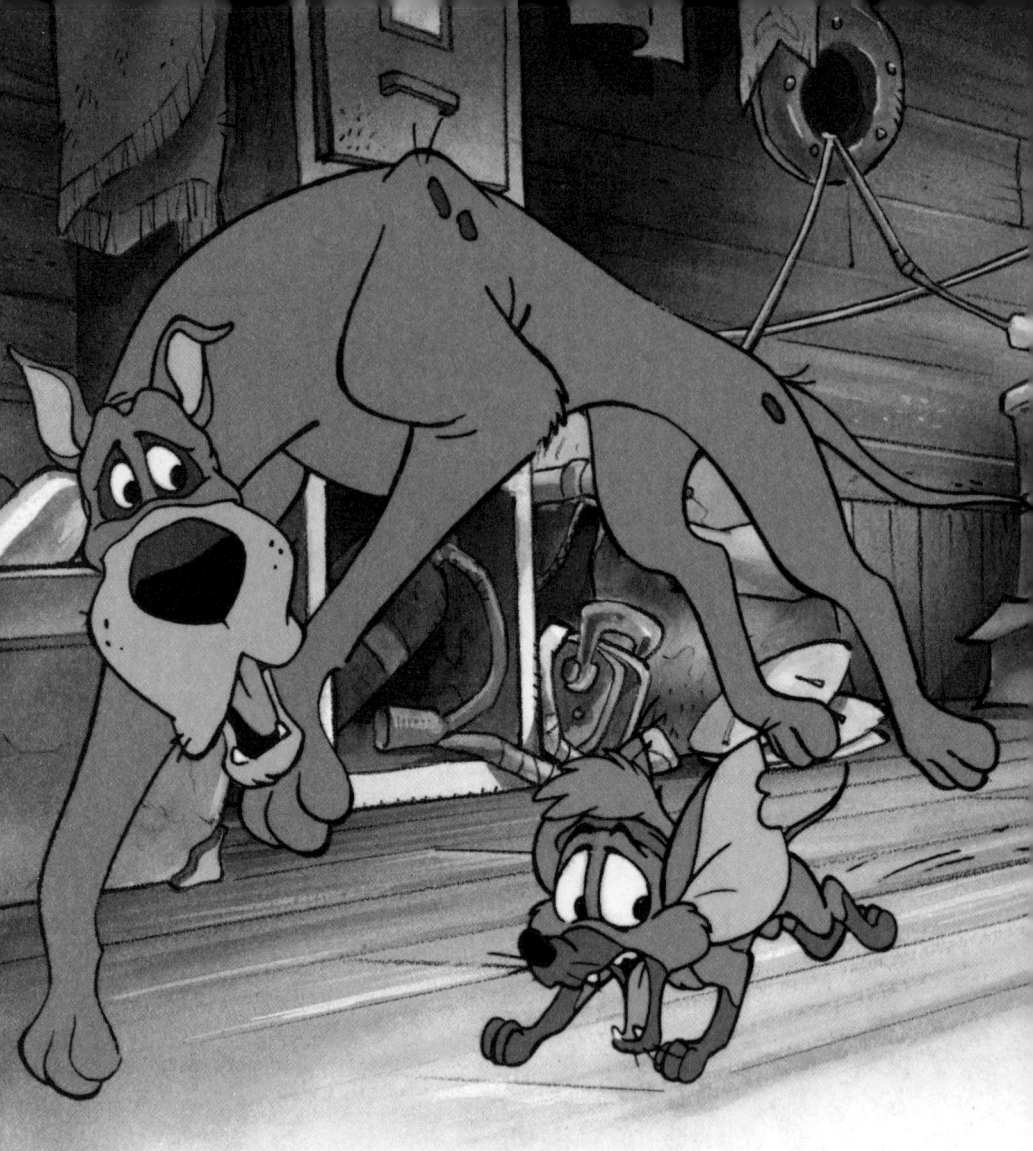

Suddenly something crashed through
the roof. The dogs looked up and then ran
for cover. "Run for your lives!" cried Tito
the Chihuahua.

"Is it the monster?" asked Rita,
a long-eared Afghan.

The kitten landed in the middle of the room with a thud! This certainly was not the monster that the dogs had expected.

"What do you want?" growled Francis the Bulldog.

Then Einstein, a Great Dane, along with Tito, Rita, and Francis, growled at the kitten, too. No cat had ever dropped in before!

"Yeah. What do you want?" snarled Rita.

"I want my share of the sausages that Dodger stole from me!" said the kitten timidly.

The dogs began to laugh. "Hey, Dodger!" Tito cried. "Is this the huge monster with the razor-sharp teeth?"

"Hi, kid!" Dodger said. "What took you so long?"

Just then they heard footsteps.

"That's our friend, Fagin," the Great Dane told the kitten.

Fagin entered the room and opened an old chest. He examined everything the dogs had brought home that day.

"I can't sell this," he cried. "That crook Sykes wants money! If I don't have it, he'll throw me into the sea!"

"Well! Look at this!" said Fagin, picking up the kitten. "We've never had a cat in the gang before. Welcome!"

That night the kitten curled up with his new friends and slept very well indeed.

The next morning Fagin took the gang to the city. "Get out there and bring back some good stuff," he said.

They split up and the kitten followed Tito. On one street they spotted a driver getting out of a limousine. But they didn't see the little girl in the back seat.

"Now's our chance!" Tito said. "Follow me!"

No one saw the kitten and the tiny dog jump into the car.

"You keep watch," Tito said, "while I steal the radio."

"Steal!" cried the kitten, accidentally hitting the horn.

The loud blast sent Tito flying. "Run!" he yelled.

As the kitten was about to go, he heard a voice. "What a pretty kitten! Where did you come from?" said the little girl. "Don't be afraid. I'm Jenny."

"Look, Winston," Jenny said when the driver returned. "I found a lost kitten! We must give him a home."

Tito and Dodger watched in surprise as the car and their new friend disappeared down the street.

It wasn't long before they drove up to a beautiful house on Fifth Avenue.

Jenny took the kitten inside and gave him a bowl of food.

"I'm going to love taking care of you," she said.

The kitten soon grew to like his new home. He and Jenny played the piano together. One day Jenny even gave him a fancy collar. "It's time you had a name," she said. "I'm going to call you Oliver."

Meanwhile Fagin and the dogs couldn't stop thinking about the kitten. "I must be getting soft," said Dodger sadly. "I really liked the little fellow." "He was sweet," said Rita, "for a cat, I mean."

"It's all your fault, Tito!" snapped Dodger. "If you had been more careful, he wouldn't have been kidnapped!"

"How can it be *my* fault?" cried Tito.

"Let's stop bickering," said Rita, "and find the kitten!"

So they all set out for the city.

The dogs searched everywhere. They finally picked up the kitten's scent in front of Jenny's house. "Look!" whispered Tito. "There's a window open up there!"

Dodger climbed through the window and found Oliver fast asleep.

Being careful not to wake anyone, Dodger slipped an empty pillowcase over the kitten and carried him outside.

When they arrived home, Fagin saw the kitten's collar. "So your name is Oliver," he said. "And the address on this fancy tag means you're living in a rich neighborhood."

Later that night Oliver told Dodger all about Jenny and said he wanted to go back. "She loves me very much," he said. "And I miss her."

Meanwhile Fagin had an idea. He wrote a letter and told the dogs to take it to Jenny's house. When the letter arrived, Jenny's parents were out, so the girl read it herself.

Dear Rich People,
We have your cat, Oliver! If you want to see him again, bring lots of money to the docks tonight!

Jenny grabbed her piggy bank and rushed to the docks. She was determined to get Oliver back that night—even though she'd never been out alone after dark before.

Fagin and the dogs were waiting on the dock. Fagin was shocked when he saw that Jenny was only a child. He knew that kidnapping Oliver was wrong and felt bad about it. So he handed Oliver to Jenny, saying, "I found this kitten. Is it yours?"

Fagin was interrupted by the roar of a huge car speeding toward them.

It was Sykes! As he drove past, he slowed down and dragged Jenny and Oliver into the car!

"Let me go!" cried Jenny, struggling with Sykes. "Oh, no!" said Sykes with a cruel laugh. "I'm going to sell you back to your rich parents."

Oliver had heard enough! He jumped out of Jenny's arms and bit Sykes on the thumb.

Sykes was so surprised that he let go of Jenny's arm. When he did, she scrambled out of the car through the sunroof.

Fortunately, Fagin and the dogs were right behind them. At Fagin's signal, Jenny jumped into his arms.

Inside the car, Sykes was furious.

He dangled Oliver in front of his vicious guard dogs.

When Dodger saw what was happening, he jumped into Sykes's car.

Although Sykes's dogs were stronger than Dodger, he attacked them before they could hurt Oliver.

As the dogs battled, Sykes lost control of the car. It crashed through a guard rail and plunged into the water!

Jenny, Fagin, and the dogs rushed to the broken railing. They looked for signs of their friends, but only bubbles floated to the surface. "I'm sorry," Fagin said sadly. "This looks like the end for Oliver and Dodger."

It was the end for Sykes and his horrible dogs, too.

Just then, Jenny saw something in the water. "It's Dodger and Oliver!" she cried happily.

Dodger had escaped and pulled Oliver to safety. Fagin petted Dodger, and Jenny hugged Oliver.

The following day was Jenny's birthday. Winston decorated the house, and Jenny invited her new friends to help her celebrate. Fagin was a new man. His worries had disappeared with Sykes.

"We'll never have to steal again," said Fagin. "Sykes's evil days are over."

Jenny couldn't imagine a happier birthday. And Oliver couldn't believe his good fortune. At last, he had a home and wonderful friends.